Mermaid Mary Margaret

Mermaid Mary Margaret

by Lynn E. Hazen

Published by Bloomsbury, New York and London
Distributed to the trade by Holtzbrinck Publishers

Library of Congress Cataloging-in-Publication Data
Hazen, Lynn E.
Mermaid Mary Margaret / by Lynn E. Hazen
p. cm.
Summary: Eleven-year-old Mary Margaret takes a cruise through the Greek Isles with her recently widowed grandmother and keeps a journal of her adventures.
ISBN 1-58234-869-3 (alk. paper)
[1. Cruise ships—Fiction. 2. Mermaids—Fiction. 3. Grandmothers—Fiction. 4. Widows—Fiction. 5. Greece—Fiction. 6. Diaries—Fiction.] I. Title.
PZ7.H314977 Me 2003
[Fic]—dc21
2002036675

First U.S. Edition 2004

Printed in Great Britain by Clays Ltd, St Ives plc

1 3 5 7 9 10 8 6 4 2

Bloomsbury USA Children's Books
175 Fifth Avenue
New York, New York 10010

All papers used by Bloomsbury Publishing are natural, recyclable products made from wood grown in well-managed forests. The manufacturing processes conform to the environmental regulations of the country of origin.

Oceans of love and appreciation to my mom and dad
for that first typewriter and a lifetime of encouragement;
fathomless thanks to Victoria Wells Arms and my critique
buddies young and old, near and far; joyful splashes to all
the kids who've inspired and continue to inspire me; and
all of the above, with love, to my three mermen—
now will you read it?
—L. E. H.

THE JOURNEY BEGINS

My New Journal

All about me,
Mary Margaret.
Mermaid Mary Margaret.

Floating

When I was in Mom's belly I floated and could hear the soothing, sloshing sounds of water. I wonder if all mermaids can remember. Is that why we love the water so much?

Mom says I must have been affected by the Water Walk class she took when she was pregnant with me. *That's* why I like to swim and splash so much. *That's* why I want to be a mermaid. She says there's no way I could remember before I was born. Or, Mom says, I watched that mermaid video one too many times, and it went to my brain. She says I should get real and pay attention to my schoolwork, or I'll never make it to fifth grade.

Maybe I'm not a mermaid right now. But I might have been one in a former life. Or maybe I'll be one in my next life.

My Catholic school doesn't have a class on past lives and future lives. And Sister Elizabeth doesn't like it when I ask too many questions. Especially questions about mermaids. I don't see why mermaids can't be included in God's many creatures. Mom says, "Mary Margaret, you ask too many questions."

Maybe it all started when Grandpa gave me that glittery mermaid toothbrush. I still have it even though the bristles are worn down. It helps me remember him.

Maybe it all started when I saw that beautiful mermaid ice sculpture at the Seniors' Seafood Buffet at Grandma's retirement village in Miami.

Wednesday Morning, April 9: Flying to Greece

I'm going with Grandma on this trip to the Greek islands so she'll start to feel better. We said good-bye to Mom and Janie in Miami (latitude: 25° 77' N, longitude: 80° 21' W), then we flew to New York (latitude: 40° 43' N, longitude: 74° 0' W). I had told Sister Elizabeth I would practice latitude and longitude. I turned in an extra-credit report because even though it's spring break I'll miss an extra three days of school. That's okay with me.

Janie is not such a bad big sister. She is in seventh grade now, and she helped me look up all the latitudes and longitudes on the Internet before I left. From New York, we've been flying and flying over the ocean to Athens, Greece. I am hoping we'll see some mermaids on this trip.

** See my report at the end of this journal for more about latitude and longitude.*

Mom couldn't come along because she had to work, and Janie couldn't come because she had important things happening at school, and a party she wanted to go to. Besides, there was just one extra ticket, Grandpa's ticket.

Grandma let me sit by the window. Part of the flight was all clouds, but sometimes I can see the deep blue of the ocean. If I had brought Grandpa's binoculars, I could have watched for mermaids.

I wish Grandpa were here. Well, I guess he is. Kind of. Not really. I don't want to think about that.

I was not even supposed to be on this trip. It was supposed to be just Grandma and Grandpa together on their dream cruise to celebrate their fiftieth wedding anniversary. They were planning it for a long time.

Grandpa told Grandma that if he didn't get better, she should still go on their dream cruise.

No binoculars. No mermaids. No Grandpa. Just a long flight. I've had three sodas, a really awful chicken sandwich, and two bags of strange crackers that were *not* peanuts.

When Grandma and Grandpa used to take vacations, they always brought me bags of airplane peanuts. Those tasted good; crunchy, salty, and sweet. Airplane crackers are not my favorite.

Grandma said, "Most airlines don't serve peanuts anymore."

Things have changed.

Grandma needs Rest, Relaxation, and Recuperation. Mom made me memorize that before we took off. Then she gave me a kiss and said, "Bon voyage." That's what people say when you go on a trip. Janie said, "Bon voyage," too. I am sure she didn't know what I had in my suitcase. Well, it's too late to give it back now.

I think Mom wants me to write in my journal so I don't talk Grandma's ear off. Mom said if I write in my journal every day, it'll give Grandma a break. From me.

This journal and the glittery pens Mom gave me are cool. Mom said my journal is just for me. Like a secret diary. Private. No one else can read it unless I want to show them. Mom said my journal is very special. Like me, she said. She said not to rip out any pages even if I didn't like what I wrote. Because the pages are sewn in and if you rip out one page, other pages will fall out later.

I keep rubbing my hands over the blue cloth cover and feeling the embossed wave on it. Mom knows I love the water. I miss her already. At the airport she gave me the best hug, then a kiss on my forehead and a gentle tug on both my braids like she does. Then she looked right into my eyes, and said, "Be good and watch over your grandma."

Days 1 and 2 in the Greek Islands (Latitude: 38° 02' N, Longitude: 23° 42' E)

Thursday, April 10: Athens

Grandma looks tired and older today. And sad. Maybe she's tired because of the long flight to Athens. Whenever I ask her anything, she answers with just one or two words, like "Hmmm" or "Maybe." We have a day to rest here in Athens before boarding the ship tomorrow. Then we start our cruise of the Greek islands.

Grandma likes looking at the guidebook and our tour plans. The ship will take us from Athens around these Greek islands: Hydra, Santorini, Crete, and Rhodes. Then back to Athens. The places we visit are called ports of call.

Grandma's sleeping a lot. Good. Rest, Relaxation, Recuperation.

I wonder if Mom told Grandma about my journal being private. I hope so. If I tell her it's private, she'll think I wrote something weird and want to sneak a peek. Maybe not. I don't know. I don't think Grandma's thinking about my journal.

Friday, April 11, 2:15 p.m.: Aboard Ship

This ship is huge and fancy. Our room and bathroom are small but perfect. We have a round porthole window. We unpacked our suitcases. I have my own little dresser, which is good, because I get nervous and sad when I see the other cabinet and remember what's in it.

We practiced putting on our life jackets in case the ship sinks. Mermaids need to know these things. Then we got a tour of the ship. Wow!

Ship lunch is a thousand times better than airplane lunch. So much food. So fancy. I am so full. The Shiny Jewelry Lady who sat at our table said I had a healthy appetite. She was covered in diamonds and had a healthy appetite too.

There are mostly old people on the ship. I haven't seen a single kid yet. Not even at the swimming pool on the upper deck. Grandma made me put on a ton of sunscreen. So far I have the pool pretty much to myself.

The ship floats along, making ripples, waves, and splashes through the ocean water. I floated in the pool, looking up at the sky. I made ripples, waves, and splashes, and did flips. I love the way it feels to twirl around in the water with my arms strong on the top, making swirling waves in circles around me. Do mermaids feel strong that way too?

Seagulls float above me through the sky. One seagull is looking at me looking at it. The sun shines down, but it is not quite as hot as in Miami. My cheeks are warm from the sun. When I squint through the droplets of water on my eyelashes, I can see that seagull in tiny rainbows.

I tried to get Grandma to come in and float. She said, "Maybe later, dear heart."

When she says, "Maybe later," that means no. She was busy looking at the guidebook and looking sad. She would have felt better if she had come in and floated with me.

Grandma is taking a lot of naps, and she doesn't let me stay in the pool when she does. I can't go back in the pool until she wakes up. Grandma told me to read the guidebook or write in my journal. She said I could go to the bathroom but nowhere else until after her nap.

I wrapped my big towel really tight around my belly and hips, all the way down my legs. Just my feet stick out the bottom. It is cozy and warm. I am a mermaid writing in my journal. I asked Grandma if she wanted to write something too, but she just shook her head.

Maybe if they had just let me be a mermaid in the school play, I would have gotten it out of my system.

Sister Elizabeth tells us in school, "Boys and girls, you can become whatever you want in this world." Then she told me I couldn't be a mermaid in the school play. No mermaids in the Bible. No two-by-two mermaids swimming along with Noah's ark.

She asked me if I wanted Father O'Reiley to answer my questions about why mermaids and reincarnation aren't real.

No, thank you. I just wanted to be a mermaid in the school play.

Noah's ark looked pretty plain in my Bible stories book. Nothing like this ship.

Grandma is sleeping in the deck chair next to me. My hair is nearly dry already, even though it is still in two long braids. Mom usually brushes and braids my hair. I did it myself today.

Angel Hair

Ashley's usually my best friend. When Ashley and I were in kindergarten after-school care, we made paper angels to decorate the day care center. I drew my paper angel with red hair like me. Then Ashley told me my paper angel wasn't a real angel. She said real angels only had blond hair.

I said, "Nuh-uh," and she said, "Yeah," back and forth, louder and louder, until Mrs. M. came over and asked what was wrong.

I asked if it was true. "Do angels only have blond hair?"

Mrs. M. said she'd never seen a real angel. But she thought that angels would probably be a lot like real people on earth, with all their different hair, some black, some curly, some straight, some red. I liked Mrs. M.

Then Ashley stood up and put her hands on her hips and said right to me and Mrs. M. in her singsongy, bossy voice, "Nuh-uh! I talked to God, and God told me that angels have blond hair . . . so Mary didn't draw an angel!"

I started crying.

Mrs. M. gave me a hug. She told Ashley that next time she talked to God she should listen more closely to God's answer. Mrs. M. had black curly hair.

Red Hair

Most days I like my red hair, but some days it is hard being different. Grandpa had red hair.

Ashley's hair is not as blond or curly as it used to be. She's not so bossy anymore either. Sometimes she's my best friend.

Some days Ashley doesn't have time to be my best friend because she is busy trading lunches with her new boyfriend, Brian the Brainiac. She probably eats lunch with Brian because she wants to look at his math homework. Brian's not so smart. I beat him at the geography bee when he didn't know that the longitude lines were the up-and-down ones and that the latitudes were the lines parallel to the equator.

I don't want a boyfriend, but if I ever did, he'd better have good things in his lunch, because I wouldn't want to trade food with just anybody.

Just once I'd like to let my long red hair loose and swim in the sea and be a mermaid. Mom said swimming with my hair loose would be a big mistake. She said, "Don't try it." Then she gave me one of those serious Mom looks.

I have to brush and braid my own hair on the ship because Grandma's hands get sore every day. "Part of growing old," she said this morning. I can't braid it as tightly as Mom can. I still miss Mom.

Friday, 5 p.m.: Seven Wonders of the World

Grandma and I have been reading the guidebook aloud to each other. Today we read about the Colossus of Rhodes. It was one of the Seven Wonders of the World. There was a drawing of it. The Colossus of Rhodes was a huge sculpture of Helios, the sun god, guarding the harbor. He was made out of melted-down weapons, and it took twelve years to build him. That's more years than my age. I wish I could have seen it, but it fell down in an earthquake.

He fell apart under the water, so I bet mermaids can still see him. We are going to Rhodes in a few days.

Maybe I will ask the recreation director to teach me how to snorkel in the swimming pool. It says Snorkeling Class on a sign by the pool, but most of the people just sit, walk, and sleep in the chairs. I still haven't seen any other kids.

I have my own Seven Wonders of the World:

1. I wonder if I will ever have a boyfriend.
2. I wonder if God hears me when I am praying, and if He will ever answer.
3. I wonder why Grandpa had to die so suddenly.
4. I wonder why I took my sister's bikini top and if she's noticed it is gone yet.

5. I wonder if that's stealing if you borrow without asking but plan to return it later.
6. I wonder how Grandma and I will feel when we scatter Grandpa's ashes in the sea, and if she will ever stop feeling so sad.
7. I wonder if I will ever get to wear my hair down, and swim in the sea, and be a mermaid.

Day 3 in the Greek Islands

Saturday, April 12, 10 a.m.

I didn't sleep well last night. At first it was cozy and snug and I was looking forward to good dreams of floating on the sea. Instead I had a bad dream about Janie going to school in just her bikini bottom and a towel.

Later today we are going to the island of Hydra.

Grandpa's ashes are in an urn in a cabinet in our room here on the ship. It's a little weird, but sort of reassuring too. He's kind of taking this trip with us.

Grandpa wanted his ashes scattered at sea, but I don't know if I am ready to help Grandma do that. If we have his ashes, we still have something. When we scatter his ashes, he will really be gone. I don't want to think about that.

Grandma doesn't talk about it. But I guess she's thinking about it all the time. Mostly she sits in one of the deck chairs and stares at the ocean. She carries the guidebook, but she doesn't read it. Not unless we are reading aloud to each other. She keeps her hanky with her and dabs at her eyes a lot.

The ship's chaplain sat and talked with Grandma this morning when I was in the swimming pool. I wanted to tell him, "Grandpa wasn't supposed to die." I wanted to say, "It's not fair. Especially for Grandma, but for me too. It happened so fast. And why wouldn't they even let me see him in the hospital?"

But I didn't say anything.

I'm still mad that I didn't get a chance to say good-bye. Or give Grandpa one last hug.

I wonder what the chaplain thinks about mermaids.

Saturday, 4 p.m.: Back Aboard Ship After Hydra, Greece

The island of Hydra (latitude: 37° 20' N, longitude: 23° 32' E) is kind of rocky, and they didn't give us much time to do anything except eat lunch and walk around a little. For lunch, we ate at a restaurant with stone walls.

Grandma didn't eat much of her spinach salad or her squid, so I tried them, but they were not my favorite. Maybe they weren't hers either. I have to think about what mermaids would like to eat. I am starting to make a list. Squid is not on the list.

Grandma drank coffee and said they brew their coffee very strong here. I had baklava. I will dream tonight of baklava. Sweet, crunchy, buttery layers and nuts.

MENU FOR MERMAIDS

Real airplane peanuts
Baklava
Seaweed?
Fish, but not squid

The best thing about Hydra is that there are no cars or buses. Grandma didn't want to ride a donkey or bike like everyone else, so we walked a little ways to the fishing port.

The Shiny Jewelry Lady actually rode a donkey up the hill. She sparkled all the way out of sight. Grandma says they are not real diamonds. The fake ones are called rhinestones. That lady had rhinestones on her sunglasses too, and a big smile on her face. The donkey was not smiling.

Ride-em-Cowgirl, Mrs. Rhinestone!

Even Grandma smiled at that. When I am a senior citizen like Grandma and Mrs. Rhinestone, I am going to ride a donkey, and scuba-dive, and maybe windsurf too.

I was hoping to walk along the shore to look for beach glass for my collection, but Grandma said we had to stay on the main road.

Back in the Cabin, 6 p.m.: Different Smells

On Hydra, the breezy air tickled my nose with the smells of stone dust, donkey doo, fishing boats, and the salty sea air, all at the same time. Our ship smells like metal, machines, and new carpets. And there is a kind of hum.

The old guy with the rocket ships on his swim trunks smells like too much aftershave. He keeps circling around Grandma and Mrs. Rhinestone, but they ignore him in a nice way.

The upper deck by the pool is best. It smells like fresh ocean air, sunscreen, and chlorinated pool water.

Last night after dinner we watched the singing show. When Miss Victoria, the main singer, walked past us toward the stage with her feather boa trailing behind her, I smelled sweet honeysuckle. Such a nice perfume, there, then gone. Miss Victoria wore a sparkling black gown and that feather boa.

I liked watching Miss Victoria sing, but Grandma was too tired to stay for the whole show. So we walked once around the upper deck and looked at the stars. Grandma likes to walk before bedtime. She says it clears her mind.

Tonight we have to dress up for dinner. Grandma had a long nap, and she says she is "as rested as I'll ever be."

Saturday Night, 11 p.m.

When Grandma is mad at me she calls me "Mary Margaret." When she is not mad she just calls me "Mary," or "Mary dear," or "dear heart." Tonight at dinner she had to remind Mary Margaret about table manners. I think she was nervous because the captain was sitting at our table. The captain has a big white mustache that curls up on both ends. It looks like he is always smiling a fuzzy, hairy smile.

I was nervous because there were so many different forks and plates and glasses, I didn't know which ones to use. Just when I thought I had it all figured out, I tried to stab a tiny cherry tomato with the proper fork and it flew over the table and landed with a splash in Mrs. Rhinestone's water glass. The captain kept smiling. Old Mr. Aftershave, who was sitting next to Mrs. Rhinestone, offered her his handkerchief. But she didn't seem interested in the handkerchief or in him.

I said, "Sorry."

Mrs. Rhinestone had so many jewels on, she must have weighed twice as much as usual.

A smiling waiter hummed and took away Mrs. Rhinestone's water glass with the tomato still bobbing around in there. That tomato looked like a happy little round beach ball bobbing in the sea.

I was thinking about that when the lady with the serious eyebrows at our table said she thought this cruise was for seniors only.

I looked at all my forks.

I wanted to ask the captain or Old Mr. Aftershave if they knew any good sea songs, but after the flying tomato incident, I thought I'd better keep quiet for a while.

After dinner we stayed and watched all of Miss Victoria's show. I get the feeling that Grandma doesn't like her very much. Maybe she thought Miss Victoria should put a sweater on or something. But when Miss Victoria sang, Grandma didn't look so sad.

If I sing one of Grandpa's songs, I wonder if it will cheer Grandma up and make her smile more, or if it will make her cry.

I love the songs Grandpa taught me, especially "Lydia, the Tattooed Lady" and "The Drunken Sailor." Mom told me not to sing them at school. Sister Elizabeth and Father O'Reiley would not like the words.

Then why does Sister Elizabeth always say, "You can be sure that God is nearby when there is a song in your heart"?

I want to sing Grandpa's songs so I won't forget the words. The songs he sang had a lot of words. I wonder if Grandma even knows them all.

No one ever talks about Grandpa's songs or his mermaid tattoo. If Grandpa were still here, *he* would talk about them. Grandpa said he got his tattoo back when he was so young and foolish that his hair was still red and he didn't know any better.

When Grandpa moved his arm, the mermaid moved too. She was very curvy. Her head, top, and arms were on his upper arm. Her tail fin was on his lower arm, with her waist near the inside of his elbow. So when he moved his muscles just right, the mermaid wiggled her hips and danced like crazy!

Maybe I will tell Janie that I took her bikini top because my hair is still red and I am too young and foolish to know any better. She'd agree with the foolish part.

The only problem is, I *do* know better. I thought

I needed it. I just borrowed it for my mermaid costume. Okay, I stole it. My green leggings were in my closet at home with my green swim fins, my beach glass collection, and my other treasures. I was going to sew some sequins and sparkly things onto my leggings, but I didn't have time. I decided the swim goggles looked too silly for my costume. And mermaids don't wear goggles, do they?

Then it was time to pack quickly for this trip, and I wanted to try out my mermaid outfit.

Mom had said, "Grandma needs you to go with her to Greece because you're brave."

Mary Margaret the Brave Red-Headed Mermaid.

Janie's bikini top was just lying there on the floor in her room.

Mary Margaret the Terrible Thief. I didn't have time to think. Now I can't stop thinking about Janie's big swim party that's coming up while I am away.

Her bikini top doesn't even fit me. Of course, it fits Janie just right. I thought I'd be able to tighten the strings on the straps, but that didn't work. Stuffing it with tissues like I saw Janie do once didn't work either. And the two ping-pong balls bounced right out!

How embarrassing. I was locked in a dressing room out by the pool, and Grandma was sound asleep in her deck chair. The ping-pong balls bounced under the door and across to the bathroom.

Poink

Ploink

Ploink

Plonk

Ploink

I stayed locked in my stall for a long time while I put my own one-piece suit back on.

Maybe I will send Janie a postcard to tell her I am sorry.

I wish Grandpa were here. He'd laugh and give me a hug and say, "It's okay to be young and foolish."

Miss Victoria

Miss Victoria has the greatest costumes! Tonight during her show, Mrs. Rhinestone and some other ladies all shook their heads and clucked their tongues, like a bunch of hens. But Miss Victoria was beautiful! Even Old Mr. Aftershave stopped flirting with Mrs. Rhinestone and watched Miss Victoria instead.

She had peacock feathers in her hair. And a sequined gown that went way down low in the back. It kept changing colors from blue to green to emerald depending on how she turned and danced in the lights. I wish I had a dress like that.

She sang a song about her love across the sea. Fake silvery foil waves went across the stage. And there was a big slit up the side of her gown . . . *way* up the side!

I told Grandma, "Those waves would be cool in our school play about Noah's ark." She just smiled. The Mean Eyebrow Lady said, "Shhh!"

I am sure if I had a chance to talk to Miss Victoria, she could give me some good advice on my mermaid costume. I wonder what she does in the daytime when she is not getting ready to perform. I'd love to sit with Miss Victoria at lunch and talk about costumes.

I wonder if Janie still loves me. I bet she hates me right now.

Day 4 in the Greek Islands

Sunday Morning, April 13, 7 a.m.: Me? A Crybaby?

Last night when Grandma brushed her hair before bedtime, she hummed a little and almost smiled. I asked her what she was thinking about.

Grandma said she was remembering when I was a baby. She said I cried a lot. "Maybe from colic," she said. "Or maybe you were just a crybaby."

She said Mom and Janie and I were living at Grandma and Grandpa's house back then. She said I hardly ever stopped crying unless I was sleeping or nursing. Grandma and Grandpa carried me around after Mom fed me, and Grandpa sang to me. But I still kept crying.

"You cried so much," Grandma said, "that your face turned as red as your hair. About the only thing that stopped you from crying was to float you gently in warm bathwater. Grandpa rolled up his sleeves, filled the kitchen sink, and cradled you, rocked you, and floated you in his big hands in that warm shallow water. Somehow the water soothed you, and you finally relaxed."

She smiled. "Maybe it was Grandpa's singing voice, or the songs he chose. Your mom and I gave you baths too, but you seemed to relax most if it was Grandpa's turn. Your little fists finally unclenched. Your eyes opened and looked up at Grandpa, and you cooed along with his songs."

Grandma said, "Dear heart, you were the cleanest, cryingest, loudest, most loved, and most bathed baby in the entire state of Florida. And did you know that's when Grandpa started calling you his sweet little Mermaid Mary?"

When she said that, my throat got all choked up tight and kind of sore. But Grandma had finally started to smile, so I had to turn away. I looked out of that little round porthole window so she wouldn't see me cry. Maybe she knew I didn't want her to.

She said, "I'm tired, dear heart." Then she turned out the light and gave me a little kiss on my head. "I'm glad you came along with me on this journey. And Grandpa would have been glad too."

When Grandma gave me that little kiss, I stopped trying to be brave. The tears spilled out and rolled down my cheeks, salty and warm. Out the window I could see the ship's lights on the water. And some stars in the sky.

It all sparkled through my tears. I bet mermaids are good at hiding their tears. Their salty tears probably just blend right into the sea. When they feel sad and look up through the ocean at night, it probably looks all sparkly to them too.

After Grandma fell asleep and I could hear her soft snore, I turned on the little light by the side table. I looked at my beach glass collection. Then I wrapped the blanket around me and started writing it all down. I don't want to forget what Grandma said. I want to remember it all.

Sunday Afternoon, 4 p.m.: Santorini, Greece (latitude: 36° 43' N, longitude: 25° 16' E)

It would be hard for mermaids to survive a volcanic eruption. But if fish and other sea creatures survived, I'm sure mermaids would have too. The tour guide said the lost city of Atlantis might be at the island of Santorini. Underwater, or buried by the volcanic eruptions.

Mermaids are smart. They must have felt the water warming up from the hot lava under the sea. They probably swam far away until it was safe to come back again.

In school we learned how to classify animals, and learned about how they live:

Feathers = birds

Hair or fur, live birth, milk to young = mammals

Whales are mammals too, and they eat plankton, I think.

Eggs, scales, reptiles, fish . . . I forget how it goes.

Mermaids have hair and definitely have you-know-what up top. But they also have scales on their big tail. I think. So are they mammals or fish or what? If I asked Sister Elizabeth, I'm sure she'd send me to Father O'Reiley again.

We took a small boat around Santorini. I tried looking for Atlantis, but the up-and-down motions made me feel a little seasick. Do mermaids ever feel seasick?

Grandma showed me Grandpa's trick of relaxed deep breathing. "Breathe in, then breathe out slowly," she said. "Concentrate on your breathing, dear heart, and you'll feel fine." It worked.

The cliffs on Santorini are tall and steep. Especially where the volcanoes blew up and the land is missing. The water is so clear, and the beaches have black sand. The little white houses go all the way up the cliffs. It looks very different from Miami.

We looked in some little shops and had lunch. I tried some of Grandma's shrimp in tomato sauce, and I let Grandma try some of my deep-fried zucchini. I wonder if mermaids like fried food, and if they ever have the chance to cook anything.

My Dad

Last night, when Grandma was snoring, I started thinking about my dad. It is strange to me that I never met him. On the way back from the island today on the little boat, I asked Grandma what he was like. She held my hand and said, "He was a nice enough guy. But kind of drifty. He liked floating around from place to place. He didn't seem too comfortable staying in any one spot, dear heart.

"He was a good dancer," she added. "Danced his way into your mom's heart. But after they got married he drove farther and farther away on his business trips."

She said he drifted to Texas one time when Janie was little and Mom was pregnant with me. He didn't seem in any hurry to head home. "Maybe that's when your mom decided it might be time for a divorce."

Janie met him, but she was so little she doesn't

remember him. Janie always says, "Who needs him? We are a family without him." That's kind of what Mom told me, but she used different words. I never thought much about my dad before. That's because I had Grandpa.

Grandpa

Grandpa collected beach glass with me, and played ball, and took me places. He taught me how to ride my bike and how to swim. Grandpa went to all the school and church parties for fathers and daughters. Our family was just right the way it was. But now Grandpa's gone.

Without Grandpa it feels like there is an empty spot. Something got torn away. Like Santorini when part of it got blasted away by the volcano. A big empty gaping spot.

I wonder if my dad in Texas ever thinks about Janie and me. Mom told me once that I could meet my dad when I turn eighteen. I don't know if I want to. I don't know if I'll be ready.

I wonder what we'll do for Father's Day this year, and how Mom will feel. Grandpa was *her* dad, so she won't have anyone to give a card to. Neither will I.

I hope Mom likes the little clay pot I bought for

her on Santorini. I miss Mom and Janie. I keep looking in all the little gift shops for something to give Janie, but nothing feels right. I hope she's not mad at me forever. With our family getting smaller, I still need Janie to be my big sister.

Dear Heart

Grandpa is the one who called Grandma "dear heart." No one calls her that anymore. I bet she misses it. I was thinking about that when Grandma was holding my hand today and telling me about my dad.

Grandma's hands are gentle, soft, and wrinkly, like her skin is one size too big. Her fingers bend a little bit to the side as if they are not quite sure which way to go. But her palms are cool and smooth. And her gold wedding ring looks so nice.

Grandma needs someone to hold *her* hand. That's going to be me.

Things to Think About

Do mermaids ever come out of the water to eat?

Why didn't Mom tell me this cruise was for seniors only? No wonder the Mean Eyebrow Lady hates me. They probably allowed me on because they felt sorry for Grandma.

How am I going to find Miss Victoria on this huge ship? How will I talk to her about my mermaid costume without Grandma finding out?

Do mermaids have their own underwater language?

Do they drink salt water? Doesn't it make them thirsty?

Do mermaids ever have to take a bath, or are they always clean from swimming in the ocean?

Did Janie go to her big swim party yet? What did she wear?

I keep trying to think about other things, but my mind keeps going back to Grandpa's ashes in the urn in our cabin. Will I be brave enough to hold Grandma's hand when we scatter Grandpa's ashes at sea?

Day 5 in the Greek Islands

Monday, April 14, 2 p.m.: Crete (latitude: 35° 29' N, longitude: 24° 42' E)

This is too funny and exciting at the same time. Mrs. Rhinestone saw a mermaid eating! Not on Crete today. Not even on this trip, but a long time ago.

We were looking at the lunch menu in the middle of our tour of Crete when she told us. I was just asking Grandma if she thought mermaids ate seafood or land food.

Grandma said, "I have no idea."

Mrs. Rhinestone kind of giggled. Then she said, "The only mermaid I ever saw was eating a hamburger."

A hamburger?

Mrs. Rhinestone laughed, and the rhinestones on her sweater jiggled up and down.

Even Grandma looked curious. I had a ton of questions then. Where was this mermaid? What did she look like? Were there other mermaids there? Did they talk to each other?

Grandma said, "Mary Margaret, slow down."

When the waiter came, no one was ready to order.

"Oh dear," Mrs. Rhinestone said, "this might not be a good story to share with children."

"Please," said Grandma, "tell us about it, or she will drive us both crazy with questions." So Mrs. Rhinestone went on.

She said it was at a nightclub near Los Angeles. A place for grown-ups. No kids allowed. She said she didn't normally go to that kind of place, but her husband had friends who were having a party there.

"And it wasn't a real mermaid," she said. "She was a lady dressed up as a mermaid."

That was fine with me. I still wanted to know what her costume looked like.

The mermaid lady worked at the nightclub, and there were other mermaid ladies too. The nightclub was down some stairs, and it was dark inside. It had a special swimming pool all lit up behind the bar, with a clear glass wall, so when the mermaids swam around in there, it was like a show for the people in the nightclub.

As Mrs. Rhinestone told us the mermaid story, I thought about how I would love to go to a mermaid swimming pool like that, even if it was pretend.

Grandma laughed. "Mary Margaret," she said, "close your mouth."

It was such a good story, I guess my jaw dropped open.

Grandma told Mrs. Rhinestone, "This is the first time since we left Miami that Mary Margaret's been speechless."

Mrs. Rhinestone and I laughed too. I also think it was the first time I saw Grandma laugh like that since Grandpa died.

Mrs. Rhinestone said, "One mermaid took a break from swimming. She sat on the edge of the pool eating a hamburger."

Mrs. Rhinestone went back to looking at the menu, and I guess she thought she was done with her story. But I recovered from being speechless.

More Questions and Answers

I had a million more questions. Mrs. Rhinestone answered most of them.

Los Angeles is in California.

No, she didn't remember the name of the nightclub.

She didn't know if it's still there. It was a long time ago.

Their tail fins were green, and maybe made of rubber. A zipper went up the back to their waists.

Yes, they could swim very well with their tail fins. Yes, they looked like they were having fun.

Yes, they had to come up for air.

No, they had regular hands, no webbing between their fingers.

No, she didn't think they opened up the pool for kids in the daytime.

Yes, she thought their belly buttons were showing.

Then I asked what their costume tops looked like. But Mrs. Rhinestone kept saying she couldn't remember. I had to know so I could figure out a way to finish my own mermaid costume. Okay, I guess I pestered her too much until she told us.

No tops! Those mermaid ladies didn't wear any tops!

Mrs. Rhinestone's face turned red. I got all flustered and embarrassed.

Grandma shook her head. "No more questions, Mary Margaret. Some things, dear heart, are better left to your imagination."

Grandma was smiling big when she told me that.

"Mary Margaret," she called me, then "dear heart," one right after the other.

I will look up the latitude and longitude of Los Angeles when I get home. And now I have two things to look for when I turn eighteen. I have to look for my drifty dad in Texas. And I have to look for that mermaid nightclub in Los Angeles.

Grandma already told me she is not planning any trips to Los Angeles. And you have to be twenty-one to enter a nightclub, even if you only plan to drink a soda.

When we finally ordered lunch, Grandma had the seafood special. Mrs. Rhinestone had moussaka. I had a hamburger.

Monday, 4 p.m.: The Exploring Game

After we toured Crete, and before we went to the pool deck, I asked Grandma to play an exploring game. I wanted to explore the ship and maybe find Miss Victoria.

Grandma seemed interested in the game at first, but then she started calling me Mary Margaret the whole time. She said I kept changing the rules and disappearing, so she wouldn't play anymore!

I was feeling mad. I only changed the rules a little. So I didn't even ask Grandma if she wanted to come in and swim with me. She never comes in anyway, but I felt kind of bad about that.

I started twirling, splashing, and kicking. Mrs. Rhinestone came in the pool, and I guess I splashed her. She called me a mean little mermaid and took off her sunglasses with the rhinestones on the tips. Then she put on her rainbow swim cap and challenged me to a splash fight.

She's a great splasher! After a few minutes we were so out of breath, laughing so hard, we had to stop.

Mrs. Rhinestone said, "That was fun. But you're still a mean little mermaid, picking on an old lady like me." I think she was joking.

I was going to ask her if she had any spare rhinestones I could borrow, but she left after that. I wanted to pretend I was diving for treasures at the bottom of the pool. I bet Mrs. Rhinestone has buckets of rhinestones in her room.

Grandma gave me some nickels and pennies to dive for instead. I have to remember to never underestimate a sparkly senior citizen. If I were in a splash fight with a lot of kids, I would want Mrs. Rhinestone on my team. First she would blind the opposing team with her sparkliness, then she'd bombard them with splashes. I wouldn't want Grandma on my splash fight team. She only has enough energy to sit around and look sad.

Finally a Snorkel and Mask

The recreation director came out to see what all the splashing commotion was about. He said, "I thought you two were drowning." Then he found a snorkel and mask that were the right size, and showed me how to use them. With the snorkel I can float forever.

I could hear my own breathing and heartbeat and listen to the sounds of the splashes and waves in the pool. It was like a whole new underwater world of my own. It was perfect for being a mermaid. People sounds were muffled and far away.

I was a mermaid, and pretended I was a dolphin too. That was a little trickier, diving under the water and leaping back up. I kept swallowing water and getting it up my nose.

Grandma made me get out too soon, saying, "Mary Margaret, if you stay in any longer, you'll turn into a wrinkly prune."

I wonder if mermaids' fingers get wrinkly from

being in the water, or if their skin is different from mine.

Monday, 9 p.m.: Museum at Irakleio, Crete

In one of the museums on Crete, I saw two snake goddess figures. They held snakes and didn't wear any tops either. We saw beautiful wall paintings, called frescoes, from the Minoan Palace of Knossos. I loved the fresco with dolphins. I felt like I wanted to dive right in. The colors were warm and cool and smooth all at the same time.

If Mom would let me paint a fresco in my bedroom, we'd have to paint on the plaster when it was still wet. Janie and Mom would have to help me. That's if Janie wants to help me do anything.

I would paint dolphins and fish, and mermaids, of course. Maybe I could glue on some of my beach glass collection for treasure. If I had a fresco on my bedroom wall full of dolphins and mermaids, I'd have good dreams every night. I'd feel like the mermaid queen. If I had good dreams, I wouldn't have to think about sad things coming up the next day.

Day 6 in the Greek Islands

Tuesday, April 15: Our Second Day Near Crete

We got up and went to breakfast, but neither Grandma nor I ate very much. The chaplain came and talked to Grandma, saying the little boat was ready. It was time to scatter Grandpa's ashes.

The captain had sent a wreath of flowers and a little card. Janie and Mom sent a note and some flowers too. I don't know how those things got here all the way from Miami.

Their note said they missed us, and they loved us, and their thoughts were with us on this morning.

The Little Boat

We went off in the little boat with the chaplain and the man who drove it. Grandma sat in the front with Grandpa's urn, and I sat behind her feeling a little seasick and all alone. Finally, a little way away, we stopped. Grandma opened the urn. The chaplain said some words, and his voice was low, calm, and clear, but I don't remember anything he said.

Grandma's eyes had a sad emptiness when we let Grandpa's ashes go. The ocean was still and deep, the sky was the bluest of blues, and Grandma's eyes had pools of water in them.

I cried too. I was there with her, but she looked so all alone. I couldn't even take her hand and say, "Dear heart, it will all be okay."

I just sat there, feeling sad, sad, sad.

Out of the Calm Sadness

After Grandma put Grandpa's ashes in the sea, I was thinking how different my life would be without him. Without his songs, his laugh, or his smiling eyes.

Just when it was all calm and empty, without a sound or a ripple on the water, a dolphin leaped out. A dolphin!

The dolphin swam just slightly ahead, then looked

back at us, tilted his snout, and kind of laughed with his dolphin noise. At first Grandma and I gasped, and then we laughed. Because one minute we were wiping tears from our faces, and the next we were laughing right along with him.

The dolphin splashed some water sideways with his snout, looked at us, then dove and disappeared under the water. A silvery gray sliver of movement, then gone.

I asked the chaplain if he knew the latitude and longitude of where we were. The guy who operated the little boat had some kind of special tracking device. He called it a GPS: global positioning system.

Latitude: 35° 20' N, longitude: 25° 09' E. That's where we said good-bye to Grandpa.

The boat floated there a bit, then the chaplain asked if we wanted to toss the flowers in the water. So we did.

"Well, dear heart," Grandma said, and she sighed. Then she nodded to the chaplain and the boat operator, and they turned that little boat back toward the big ship.

As we turned around, I reached into my pocket for a handful of my favorite beach glass from Miami. Ambers, blues, clears, frosty whites, and greens.

Plinkety

Plink

Plink

Beautiful colors sinking into the sunlit sea.

Then Grandma and I sat close, and we looked back at those flowers floating on the smooth water, farther and farther away. We held hands tight. I never ever wanted to let go.

Tuesday Afternoon, 3 p.m.: Lonely Ship

When we got back on the ship, Grandma and I decided to skip the second tour of Crete. That was fine with me. I felt so tired and tender. I think Grandma did too. We ate a little, walked around the ship, and looked at the ocean.

Not many people are on the ship today because they all went to Crete. It feels kind of quiet and lonely. The hum of the ship is louder than usual, as if the ship misses everybody.

Grandma asked me if I felt like going to the pool, and for once I didn't want to. We sat on some deck chairs and Grandma dozed a little. I am just thinking, staring at the sky, and writing in my journal.

Grandma didn't eat much breakfast or lunch, so I have to make sure she eats plenty at dinner tonight.

I keep looking over the deck railing. But the water is pretty far down, and I can't see any dolphins. I am trying to think of good things that aren't too sad. Like Miss Victoria. She was beautiful as usual last night. I wish I could sing like her.

Tuesday Night, 8:30 p.m.: All My Fault

It's all my fault. Grandma said she wasn't very hungry at dinner and that her food had lost all of its flavor. She had seafood again, and I had another hamburger.

I told her she had to eat, to keep strong for our tour of Rhodes tomorrow. I pestered her until she called me Mary Margaret and finally ate some of her fish.

Then she got sick. Really sick!

It was awful. We went back to our room, and she stayed in the bathroom. I could hear her getting sick in there, and I was so scared. I still am.

I tried to get her to drink a little bit of water. She said she just needed to rest. But she looked so awful and pale, and then she kept going back in the bathroom.

When she came out again, she could hardly walk to her bed. I had to help her. Grandma said, "I need to find someone to watch over you." But she felt woozy. Her face and her hands were all sweaty, and she looked at me like she could barely see me there.

Then she started talking to Grandpa. I was afraid she wanted to go and be with him. She seemed like she was looking far, far away.

I held her hand and got a cool wet washcloth for her forehead. I called her "Grandma dear," but she didn't answer me. Her eyes were open, but she had stopped talking completely. Her lips moved a little, but no sound came out. I couldn't even tell if she was still breathing.

That was too scary, so I pushed the red button on the phone, and I said it was an emergency. They took her away on a stretcher to the ship's infirmary. I ran behind.

The doctor is looking at her now, and they are making me stay out here in the waiting room. Why won't they let me see her? I don't even want to think about that, but I can't stop thinking she is sick because of me. It is all my fault.

Tuesday Night, 10:20 p.m.: Not So Brave Mary Margaret

The nurse said, "Your grandma will be okay. It's food poisoning or some kind of stomach flu."

But Grandma didn't look okay when they took

her away on the stretcher. I wonder if Grandma can talk now. I keep asking the nurse, but she won't tell me.

The nurse said Grandma is resting and getting liquids through an IV. She said I was very brave and smart. She said, "You called just in time for us to take good care of your grandma."

If Grandma is okay, why won't they let me see her?

The nurse said I could see her in the morning *if* the doctor decides she is strong enough for visitors.

I started to cry. The nurse looked worried that she might be stuck with me. She asked, "Do you know anyone else on the ship?"

Thou Shalt Not Lie

The nurse doesn't know that Grandma is sick because of me. The nurse doesn't know I lied about who I know on the ship.

The steward with all the keys who brought me to Miss Victoria's cabin and unlocked the door doesn't know, either.

Pretty soon the whole world will know that Mary Margaret steals bikini tops and tells lies. What will Miss Victoria do when she finds me in her room?

Tuesday Night, 10:45 p.m.

When the nurse asked me who I knew on the ship, I thought of Mrs. Rhinestone, of course. But Mrs. Rhinestone is not her real name. I'm so upset about Grandma, I still can't remember her real name. Mrs. Rhinegold? Mrs. Reinholt? Why did I write Mrs. Rhinestone so many times in my journal?

That's what I was thinking, and I was still crying, when the nurse said, "Oh dear, you *must* know someone else on the ship."

And I said, "Miss Victoria." It just popped out. I didn't really mean I knew her. The nurse was so happy to get rid of me, she started talking on the phone and arranging things really fast. I was too scared to stop her.

Since Miss Victoria is in the middle of her show, the steward brought me to her room, opened the door, and left me alone in here. This room smells weird. Like old stuff. Not like Miss Victoria at all.

10:55 p.m.: A Big Mistake

I sat there, fiddling with some beach glass in my pocket when someone knocked on the door. I had to answer. It was another steward from the pharmacy.

He had some ointment for Mrs. Victoria Meddlesmith. Mrs. Meddlesmith? That didn't sound right.

"What are you doing in Mrs. Meddlesmith's cabin?" he asked. "Mrs. Meddlesmith will be furious to find you here. She just retired from being a school principal for forty years and she needs a long break from kids. She's already complained to the staff about seeing a child on board."

Everyone knew there was only one child on board: me!

Just then someone stood in the doorway glaring at me. The Mean Eyebrow Lady from the flying tomato dinner. I grabbed my journal and ran as fast as I could down the passageway and up, up, up to the top deck. I could hear them shouting after me, but I just kept running.

So I'm hiding in one of the lifeboats. I thought it would be warm and safe, but it's so cold up here. It smells like old rubber. At least there is no one else around. I need to think how to get back to see Grandma at the infirmary and how to find Miss Victoria's room. The *right* Miss Victoria!

I can't believe they left me in the wrong room, especially with that mean old Mrs. Meddlesmith!

11:05 p.m.: The Not So Brave Mermaid Mary Margaret

In the lifeboat I got all shivery. Then I felt seasick too. I tried doing Grandpa's relaxed deep breathing. I whisper-sang a couple of Grandpa's songs. I heard Mom's voice telling me I was brave. That's why she sent me along on the cruise. I needed to be brave and watch over Grandma.

I had to get back to the infirmary to make sure Grandma was okay. Grandma needed me.

I climbed out of that lifeboat and looked around until I found a map of the ship on the wall. No longitude or latitude, but it showed where the infirmary was. On the third deck below. I snuck down the stairs and kept looking until I found it.

I stayed hidden from the nurse at the desk by crouching down so she couldn't see me. I did more deep breathing to keep my heart from pounding too fast or too loud. When she finally went down the hall to the bathroom, I peeked behind the curtain.

There was Grandma. She was asleep, and I could hear her soft snoring. She looked so pale and weak on that small bed with the white sheet up to her chin. A needle with a tube went into one of her arms. A clear bag was hanging from a metal pole nearby, and something was drip-drip-dripping slowly into Grandma's arm.

I tiptoed to the other side of her bed and held her hand. They had taped her wedding ring around her finger.

"Grandma, please be okay," I whispered. "I'm trying to be brave, Grandma."

Grandma kept sleeping. I listened to her breathing. I sang her "Amazing Grace," very quietly, because I know she likes that song.

Just when I was putting some beach glass on the little table next to the bed so Grandma would know I had visited her, the curtain swooshed open and the nurse found me. She said I couldn't stay with Grandma, even though there was an empty chair right there.

Finally the Right Room?

The nurse called the steward with all the keys, and this time he took me to the right room. Anyway, I think it's the right Miss Victoria's room. He promised me it was, and he said he wouldn't make the same mistake twice.

"Stop crying," he said. Then he closed the door and left me all alone in here on her little green couch.

Before I was worried about Grandma. Now I'm worried about Miss Victoria too. Is this really her cabin? And what will she do when she finds a strange child in her room?

At least it smells nice, like honeysuckle on a warm day in Grandma's garden. But I will not get up and look around her room. I am not a snoop.

I couldn't help myself. It was so dark I had to turn on another light. Next to the lamp on the table were some photos. I wasn't exactly snooping . . . just looking. I wonder who the man is in all the photos. He's in a lot of them, especially the ones at the beach.

What if Miss Victoria is really a Mrs.? I'd better check the closet to see if a man's clothes are in there. And maybe there's room for me to hide.

How did I get myself into this? If Grandma could still talk, she would call me Mary Margaret for sure.

Hiding

Miss Victoria found me in her closet. She was calling my name: "Mary, Mary, where are you?" She knew I was hiding somewhere. Someone must have told her I was there.

When she opened the closet door, I screamed. Then she screamed. Then I started crying and saying, "I'm sorry."

Miss Victoria said, "It's okay, Mary, come out."

We sat on her little green couch, and she asked me if I was okay, but I wasn't.

Nothing was okay.

Grandpa died and his ashes were in the sea, and Grandma was sick, and it was all my fault, and I missed my mom, and I was a thief, and a liar, and a mean little mermaid, and they left me all alone in the Mean Eyebrow Lady's cabin, and Grandma couldn't even talk, and what if she didn't get better? And I prayed and I prayed but God never answered.

Miss Victoria patted my back and listened.

I don't know how she understood me. I cried so much that she gave me a hanky, then a whole box of tissues. Then she ordered some chamomile tea from room service, and then some oranges and cookies. But I couldn't eat or drink, so she left it all on the table, and I just cried and cried, and I told her everything. Well, almost everything.

She said, "Your grandma will be okay," and she offered to have me sleep in her bed, but I said no, that was her bed.

So she made me a cozy spot on her little green couch, and she sang me a song and tucked me in with a soft fuzzy blanket, and I finally stopped crying, but sniffles came out, and a big gulp now and then.

"I'm sorry I lied about knowing you," I said. And she said she *did* know me.

"You're the only red-haired little girl on the ship

who sits at the front table while I sing every night. And when you weren't there, I had to come looking for my best fan. It will all be okay, and we'll check on your grandma together in the morning.

"You must be tired from such a long, busy day. It's late," she said, "so sleep, and please don't wake me till ten in the morning, because I need my beauty rest. And since you shared so many secrets," she said, "I'll tell you a secret tomorrow too. But first, let's sleep."

She rubbed my back and sang me another song, and I tried Grandpa's relaxed breathing. I felt so tired and my eyes burned, and Miss Victoria wouldn't lie, and her voice was soothing, and she smelled like honeysuckle in Grandma's garden on a summer day, so maybe Grandma really was okay, so then I was finally okay. And I fell asleep on her little green couch.

A New Day, Day 7, in the Greek Islands

Wednesday, April 16, 9 a.m.

I woke up early, tiptoed to the bathroom, washed my face, and tried to brush my hair with my fingers. When I looked in the mirror I looked different, but I didn't know why.

Miss Victoria is still sleeping. I've been sitting here on her little green couch, writing in my journal. I am trying to write down everything that happened last night.

I was hungry, so I ate all the oranges and cookies, and drank the cold tea. I hope that's okay. I'm nearly sure she got it all for me.

Miss Victoria is beautiful even when she is sleeping.

She smiles a half smile and she breathes softly. Maybe she is dreaming about mermaids.

The way she smiles in her sleep, I'm sure her secret is a good one. Just half an hour more and I'll wake her up.

Grandma, 11:30 a.m.

When we went to the infirmary, Grandma told Miss Victoria, "Thank you for taking good care of my Mary Margaret." Then Grandma held both of Miss Victoria's hands and looked deep into her eyes, like she does sometimes. "It's nice to meet you up close," Grandma said.

Miss Victoria smiled and said, "The pleasure is all mine."

Grandma hugged me, and I helped her sit up. She told me, "Your beach glass cheered me up this morning, dear heart. But not as much as seeing your precious face."

Grandma can talk just fine now.

The nurse promised me that Grandma is going to be okay. She just needs to rest up in our cabin for a day. I am still worried, though. Grandma still looks pale and tired, and that nurse doesn't always get things right.

Miss Victoria talked to Grandma about tomorrow. They made me wait out in the hall while they discussed things. This morning Miss Victoria told me her secret. It feels like a dream. I don't even want to write about it yet. I'm so excited just thinking about it. I hope Grandma agrees.

Wednesday Afternoon: With Mrs. Rhinestone on Rhodes (latitude: 36° 24' N, longitude: 28° 15' E)

Since Grandma needed to rest up and Miss Victoria is so busy, Mrs. Rhinestone asked Grandma if she could borrow me for the day.

At first I didn't want to leave her, but Grandma said she needed to sleep as much as possible. She said it would be easier to sleep if our cabin was totally quiet. I told her I could stay on the ship on the upper deck by the pool while she slept, but she said that she wanted me to see the statue of Aphrodite on Rhodes.

Grandma said, "Your grandpa and I really wanted to see that statue, but I'm plumb worn out. Could you please do my looking for me, dear heart, and tell me all about it when you get back?"

They took out her IV, and Mrs. Rhinestone and I walked with Grandma back to our room. When she was all settled in, she shooed us out. "Let me rest now, dear heart," she said.

Miss Victoria is going to Rhodes today too, but not with us. She is going with Lucy, the hairdresser on the ship, and with some other ladies.

They're going to the Turkish baths. I wish I could go with them. Tomorrow I will see Miss Victoria again, and Lucy too, but we won't have time to go to the Turkish baths.

If Grandma feels better tomorrow, the two of us will go back to Rhodes, but not to any more museums.

Aphrodite, Goddess of the Sea and Love

I am too excited. I will make myself think about the statue to keep calm about tomorrow.

Mrs. Rhinestone and I took another little boat to Rhodes. We saw museums and walked around the Old Town with its thick old walls, gates, and archways. And of course we ate lunch. Hamburgers for both of us. I was practically skipping the whole day because I am so excited about tomorrow.

The Aphrodite of Rhodes was smooth and gorgeous. She had no clothes on. Lots of these statues and paintings don't. I'm usually embarrassed to look at them naked, but the Aphrodite of Rhodes looked so gentle, I had to stop and stare.

Mrs. Rhinestone said, "Isn't she lovely? Aphrodite was the goddess of the sea. And the goddess of love."

No wonder she was so beautiful.

The Aphrodite of Rhodes was kneeling down and lifting her long wavy hair. You couldn't tell what color it was, because she is all smooth white marble. But I imagined she had red hair, like me. As the goddess of the sea, I bet Aphrodite knew lots of mermaids.

Her body looked beautiful too. She had strong legs like me. I bet that helped her swim in the ocean with all her sea creature friends. Mrs. Rhinestone let me look at all the things I wanted, then let me go back and look at the Aphrodite of Rhodes again.

Even though she's not invited tomorrow, Mrs. Rhinestone helped me choose a present for Miss Victoria in Old Town. It's a fancy white lace tablecloth. I bought Grandma a little lace hanky too.

Mrs. Rhinestone said, "Your grandma is lucky to have such a sweet and funny granddaughter." Mrs. Rhinestone is very nice to me, as long as I don't splash her.

Mrs. Reinherz, Mrs. Reinherz, Mrs. Reinherz. There, now I will never forget it. Mrs. Rhinestone's real name is Mrs. Reinherz.

She told me, "Reinherz means 'pure heart' in German." I'll still call her Mrs. Rhinestone in my journal, because I like all her sparkliness, but I am glad I wrote down her real name too.

Wednesday, 4:30 p.m.: About Tomorrow

I have to write it all down.

I am too excited.

I can't wait anymore.

When Miss Victoria gets married tomorrow, she wants me to be her flower girl. She wants me to be her mermaid flower girl! For her beach wedding on Rhodes!

Dmitri is her fiancé's name. He's the guy in the beach photos I saw. He's even handsomer in real life, Miss Victoria said. Dmitri's a baker on this ship, and his family has a bakery on Rhodes too.

He has tons of family and friends to come to the wedding, but Miss Victoria's family is all back in the United States. That's why Miss Victoria was so happy to invite Grandma and me to her wedding tomorrow.

When I was crying last night and blubbering about everything, I guess I told Miss Victoria about Janie's bikini top and my unfinished mermaid costume. This morning Miss Victoria told Grandma and me that a mermaid flower girl would be perfect for her beach wedding tomorrow, and Grandma said,

"Yes, that would be fun."

Grandma said *yes*!

Miss Victoria gave me the absolutely most perfect shimmery scarf that I can use as a top for my mermaid costume. It matches one of her gowns. She said I could *keep* it.

It's long, stretchy, and shimmery, and changes colors in the light, just like the gown she wore that night she sang with the fake waves, when she had all the peacock feathers in her hair.

Miss Victoria wrapped the long scarf around my chest two times, which makes my chest look bigger. I have been waiting a long time for that.

I showed Grandma how I looked in my costume, and Grandma smiled really big. She got a little nervous with my long fins bumping into everything. Grandma said I might not want to wear them when I am walking on the sand. But I am sure it will be easier to walk on the beach.

We'll see Miss Victoria again tomorrow morning. I can hardly wait. I am so excited, I want to stand on the table and dance and sing Grandpa's "Lydia the Tattooed Lady" song. But Grandma is napping again, so I just have to write quietly in my journal and sing and dance on the inside of my head. Inside my head, Grandpa is singing and dancing along with me.

Wednesday Night, 11:30 p.m.: Can't Sleep

Grandma's cheeks are getting a little rosy again. She didn't eat as much as Mrs. Rhinestone at dinner, and she skipped the seafood entirely, but I think Grandma is feeling a little better.

After dinner tonight, Grandma said, "Mary Margaret, you are making me nervous with all your jumping around." So Mrs. Rhinestone borrowed me again.

We walked Grandma back to our cabin so she could rest. Then Mrs. Rhinestone took me to the ship's library. I didn't even know the ship had a library. The library had dark wood tables, thick red and gold carpeting, and fancy green glass lamps. I would love to find some beach glass in that color someday.

Mrs. Rhinestone said she noticed I liked Aphrodite at the museum today, so she wanted to show me a book she found in the library. It had a photo of the Aphrodite of Rhodes we saw today, and some other statues, drawings, and paintings too.

There were other Greek goddesses, so I wrote them down: Athena, Demeter, Hera, Hestia, Artemis, and the nine Muses.

My head is full of so many ideas and images, I feel like I am dreaming, only I still can't fall asleep. I like hearing Grandma's soft snore, breathing in, breathing out. I have to turn off the light and try to sleep.

Like Miss Victoria, I need my beauty sleep. Especially since tomorrow I will be Mary Margaret the Mermaid Flower Girl!

Day 8: Romantic Rhodes

Thursday Morning, April 17

Grandma woke me up for an early breakfast, but I was too excited to eat very much.

I wore my mermaid costume with sandals instead of my swim fins. We brought Miss Victoria's wedding present. Grandma liked the lace tablecloth. I knew she would.

A smaller boat took us to Rhodes. Then we walked to the hotel near the beach where some of the wedding guests are staying. Miss Victoria and Lucy and some other ladies were getting ready at the hotel.

Lucy fixed my hair, brushing it all out three or four times. She liked that I was a mermaid flower girl, so she said she'd make my hair wavy like the ocean.

Grandma said, "Fine, that would look lovely."

Lucy sprayed my hair with some sweet-smelling stuff, then braided it in about four or five big braids with curlers at the ends, and three long clips from my part to my ears on each side. Then she put me under a hair dryer and fixed Grandma's and Miss Victoria's hair too.

When my hair was dry, Lucy took out the braids, curlers, and clips, and it was really wavy. She combed it out very gently so it was smooth but kept the waves. Then she wove in green and silver ribbons and a few big glass beads. I pretended I had seaweed and treasures in my hair. Grandma took some pictures while Lucy misted me with some sparkly hair spray.

I was hoping Grandma would let me wear makeup. But Grandma said, "Mary Margaret, brightly colored makeup is not becoming for girls your age."

Miss Victoria said, "Your grandma's right. You look beautiful just as you are, especially with your freckled face kissed by the sun."

That made me smile.

Lucy dabbed sparkle gel on everybody's cheeks. Even on Grandma and me.

Miss Victoria said, "The grandma of the mermaid flower girl needs to sparkle too."

Grandma smiled big at that and said, "Oh my gosh!"

They gave me a little basket with some flowers and seashells, and I put some of my Miami beach glass in there too. Grandma kept my green swim fins in her straw basket. She was right about how hard it was to walk in them.

Grandma and I went out to the beach, where the wedding guests were already starting to gather. Miss Victoria and Lucy would come a few minutes later.

Grandma said, "Don't be nervous, dear heart. You look lovely. This is going to be fun."

As soon as she told me, "Don't be nervous," my hands got sweaty, and I had to keep wiping them on my green leggings. I made Grandma check the knot on my mermaid top three times to make sure it wasn't coming undone. I did *not* want to be like one of those mermaids with no tops in Los Angeles!

More and more people started to gather on the beach. Some were dressed up fancy, and others wore casual clothes like shorts and Hawaiian-style shirts.

Theo

There were lots of kids running around. Some little kids, and some kids like me, and some older teenagers too.

Dmitri and his nephew Theo came to talk to us.

Theo must have been exactly my height because our eyes were right at the same level, though his hair was sticking up all over the place, and that made him look a little taller. Dmitri explained how I would sprinkle the flowers and seashells as I walked up the beach, and Theo would carry the rings until they needed them. Dmitri said Theo was just beginning to learn English in school but that he didn't speak much yet.

I looked at Theo, and he gazed right at me with his dark brown eyes, the longest eyelashes, and his wild curly hair. He gave me a silent smile that started like a small pebble dropped in water, spreading wider and wider. Wow, what a smile. Then Theo touched my hair and said, "Red, beautiful."

And oh my gosh, my face felt hot and my heart was pounding.

Luckily it was time to get started.

Flowers and Beach Glass

Someone played violin music, and the people all gathered around. Grandma gave me a little kiss, then nudged me forward.

I sprinkled the flowers and seashells from my basket as I walked. At first Theo was behind me, then he stood next to me with a huge nervous grin like he was having fun, but also like he would rather be somewhere else at the same time.

The violin music changed, and Miss Victoria walked forward with her long dress and lacy veil, and Lucy as her bridesmaid. I couldn't have dreamed up a better wedding. The sun was shining and the sea was right there. It was romantic, and I was a part of it all. I was Mary Margaret the Mermaid Flower Girl!

Theo dropped one of the rings in the sand, and I had to help him find it. Then the chaplain and the priest said some words in English and in Greek. Miss Victoria and Dmitri put the rings on each other and kissed. Then they kissed some more.

Everybody was smiling and clapping and hugging and congratulating them. And then—and then—I couldn't believe it.

Right in the middle of all that, Miss Victoria and her new husband whipped off their fancy wedding clothes, and underneath they were wearing matching swimsuits. Bikini swimsuits in the same bright blue and purple print.

We were so surprised. Not just at how small Dmitri's swimsuit was, but because Miss Victoria and Dmitri ran to the water and dove right in. They started swimming and splashing and laughing and calling everyone to join them. And lots of people did. I guess some people knew in advance, because they were already wearing swimsuits under their clothes too.

I looked at Grandma and she said, "Go for it, Mermaid Girl."

When I reminded her I hadn't brought my suit, she said, "Mermaids are drip-dry, it is plenty sunny, and you will dry out soon enough."

Grandma also said, "You only live once."

She took some photos of my perfect mermaid costume. Theo jumped in some of the photos too, smiling that smile. Then he took my hand and said, "Yes, yes, come swim."

When I finally got to the water, I took a deep breath. I wanted that moment to last forever. Then I walked slowly into the water up to my knees and dove in.

I was Mermaid Mary Margaret swimming in the sea! My hair floated for a second, thick, loose, and sparkling on the surface of the cool water.

Theo and I smiled at each other underwater. I did some flips. He did too. Then he twirled and jumped off the sandy bottom and splashed me.

It felt so good that I half expected to see Aphrodite riding on the back of a dolphin on the next swell of waves. And maybe Grandpa riding another dolphin right behind Aphrodite, waving like the winner in a beauty contest, but with his mermaid tattoo showing on his arm as he waved. That idea made me smile and wave and slide under the surface for more watery somersaults and flips.

Theo laughed and talked to me (in Greek, I am sure) under the water.

"Bourble blup bup
rooutle
rub bup bup."

I suddenly felt that Grandpa was there too, talking to me in the sounds of the bubbling, laughing water.

I came up for a big breath of air, and I waved to Grandma back on the beach. She had taken off her shoes and was walking in the water along the shore with the chaplain. She smiled and waved at me, and the sun shone on her silvery hair. She looked beautiful, just a tiny bit sad, and not quite so lonely as before.

I floated on my back, looking up at the sky. Theo swam around and around, but I was quiet and floated there for a long while.

After Swimming: Greek Taverna on Rhodes

The wedding party moved from the beach to the taverna, and the next few hours were a fast blur. There were big platters of pastries and a three-tiered cake with a tiny bride and groom in a little boat on the top. I helped carry more pans of cookies from the bakery, smiling and saying hi to all of Theo's relatives.

There was music and Greek line dancing. Theo's legs flew every which way as he tried to teach me the steps. Grandma laughed and took photos.

Later, Theo smiled and held out another tray of cookies to me. Mermaid cookies! With tiny raisins for eyes, little dried-apricot lips, two almonds for their tops, and sesame seeds on the tails. Too pretty to eat, and still warm from the oven. I was so full that Dmitri's mom wrapped some in paper and put them gently in my basket.

Finally Miss Victoria and Dmitri cut the big cake. They fed each other tiny bites and kissed again. We all got a small piece, and it tasted so sweet and rich and good.

Then Grandma gave me a present: a little address book with a dolphin on the cover. At first I didn't understand. Then Grandma said, "You might want to get Theo's and Miss Victoria's addresses, and maybe Dmitri's family at the bakery too. We have to go now, dear heart."

She said it was getting late, and that it was time to return to the ship. My heart flip-flopped.

Good-byes

Miss Victoria thanked me for being the best mermaid flower girl ever. She wrote three addresses in my new address book: her ship address, her home in the United States, and her address on Rhodes with Dmitri.

Grandma told Miss Victoria, "Please come visit us in Miami, dear. We'll always have a place for you."

I thanked Miss Victoria for taking care of me when Grandma was sick, for the shimmery scarf for my mermaid outfit, and for letting me be her flower girl. Miss Victoria held me tight in the best hug.

Theo held my hand as we walked up the dock. No boy had ever held my hand like that before. I called to Grandma to wait a minute, and I had to let go of Theo's hand. I reached carefully into the bottom of my basket and pulled out a handful of beach glass.

When I turned toward Theo, he was frowning, until I opened one of his hands and dropped some beach glass into his cupped palm. Then he smiled and put the beach glass in his pocket.

He said, "Good-bye, Mary Mermaid." Then he kissed me really quick on my cheek.

I didn't expect that.

I ran to Grandma and we got on the little boat. I waved and waved as the boat pulled away, and Theo got smaller and smaller in the dark until I couldn't see him waving to me at all anymore.

On that little boat back to the ship, I leaned in close next to Grandma, and she hugged me and held my hand. Grandma whispered to me, "You seem to have made some really nice friends."

I whispered, "Yes."

Grandma hugged me tight and said, "We've had quite a journey together, haven't we, dear heart?"

I nodded. My heart had never felt so full. I asked Grandma, "Have you ever felt happy and sad at the same time?"

"Oh yes," Grandma said. "That's quite a feeling, isn't it?"

Late Thursday Night, 11:15 p.m.

Back on the ship, Grandma fell asleep right away. I love the sound of her soft snoring. I am so tired too, but I had to write all of this down. I don't want to forget any of it. I've been writing so much, my hand is sore, my journal is almost full, and I am getting hungry all over again.

I just peeked into my basket to unwrap a cookie to nibble. Only one was broken. But there was a surprise too. A mermaid cookie cutter!

Athens Airport: Heading Home

Saturday, April 19, 10:30 a.m.: At the Airport in Athens, Greece

I didn't get a chance to write in my journal at all yesterday. But I thought about a lot of things. Now it is Saturday, and we're waiting for our flight. Grandma has our passports and the tickets. Our bags are all checked in.

I asked Grandma if she felt like she'd had enough Rest, Relaxation, and Recuperation. "Oh yes," Grandma said. "I don't think I could handle any more of those three R's. It's time we head home."

Yesterday we went shopping and had lunch with Mrs. Rhinestone in Athens. I told her all about the wedding. Mrs. Rhinestone told us she lives in San

Francisco, and she wrote her address in my dolphin address book. Of course, she wrote her real name, Mrs. Reinherz. She said if we ever take a vacation to San Francisco, she'd love to see us.

She wrapped her big arms around us both in squishy hugs, and she gave me a little present that she made me open right there. It was a hair clip with a tiny rhinestone on it.

"Thank you, Mrs. Rhinestone!" I said. "Oops, I mean Mrs. Reinhertz!"

I was so embarrassed, and I felt my face was glowing red.

Mrs. Reinhertz laughed and said, "You are quite a unique mermaid girl, Mary Margaret. I hope we all meet again sometime."

Grandma said, "Dear heart, if this trip is any indication, you are bound to have many friends from all over the world. You'll definitely need your address book to keep track of them all."

I am going to write down all of their towns' latitudes and longitudes next to their names when I get home. I like knowing where things are in this world.

Forgiveness

I finally found a good present for Janie. Another

bikini set. Top and bottom. Grandma wanted to know how I knew her exact size, so I had to tell her the whole story. I said how sorry I was, and I asked Grandma if she thought Janie would stay mad at me forever.

Grandma said, "Maybe you should buy Janie two presents, Mary Margaret."

That was a good idea. Grandma also said it was usually hard for anyone to stay mad at me for very long. Luckily she was right. When we called home to tell Mom and Janie our flight was delayed, Janie forgave me for taking her bikini top. The swim party was canceled anyway because it was raining. They went bowling instead.

Grandma is talking more now than she was at the beginning of the trip. Last night while we were packing, we talked about Miss Victoria's wedding. Then she told me all about when she and Grandpa got married.

"All my prayers were answered," she said, "when I met and married your grandpa."

I told Grandma about all the things I prayed for. "I prayed for my hair not to be so red, and for Sister Elizabeth to let me be a mermaid in the school play, and for the right costume, and for Grandpa to stay alive. But I don't think God was listening to me, because God never answered."

"I think God hears you," Grandma said, and she

gave me a good hug.

"Me too," I said. "I think I heard God talking to me in the bubbling, laughing waves when I was swimming out there with Theo."

"So that's why you were out there so long," she said. "I thought you had finally turned into a real mermaid."

How did she know?

Mary Margaret's New Seven Wonders of the World

1. I wonder if Mom missed me.
2. I wonder what I missed at school, and where the other kids went on their vacations.
3. I wonder how much of a fuss Sister Elizabeth and Father O'Reiley will make about my new idea for the school play. A peacock! They'll have to agree there were two peacocks on Noah's ark.
4. I wonder if I can find enough feathers, and if Mom will let me wear a shimmery dress with a huge slit up the side.
5. I wonder if Theo is my boyfriend, or if you can even have a boyfriend for just one day.
6. I wonder where Grandma will go on her next big trip, and I wonder if she'll take me with her.

7. I wonder if Janie will like the journal I bought her in the airport gift shop.

I bought another journal for me too, because this one's almost all filled up. Janie's has seashells on the cover. Mine has a map of the world.

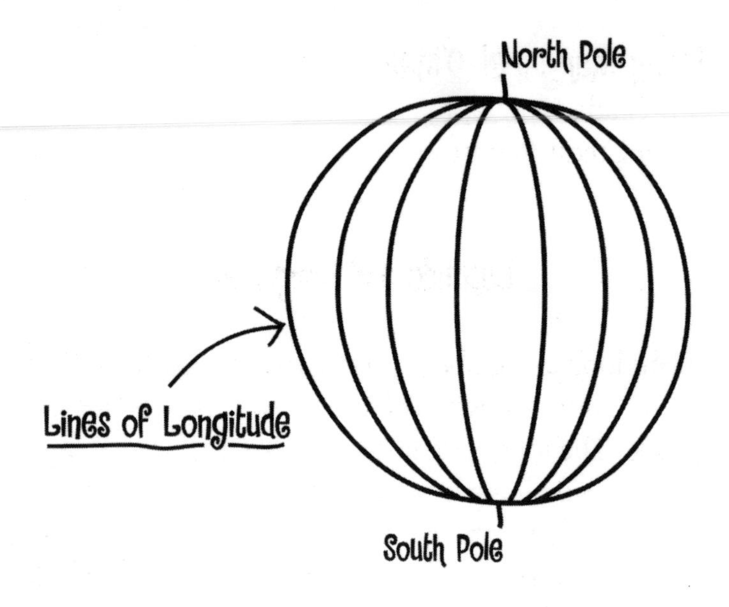
North Pole
Lines of Longitude
South Pole

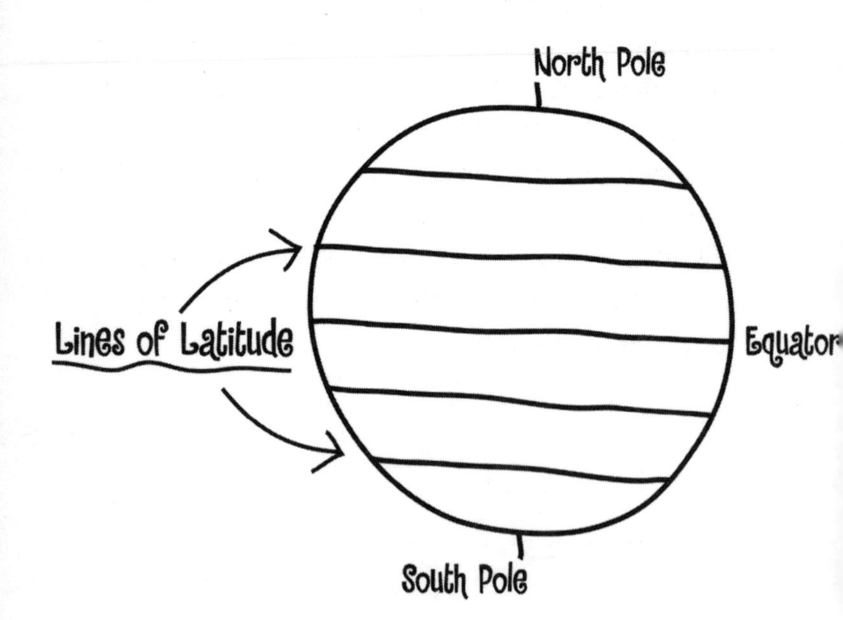
North Pole
Lines of Latitude
Equator
South Pole

Mary Margaret O'Mara

4th Grade Geography

Extra Credit Report

Latitude and Longitude

If you look at a globe or world map, you will see lines crisscrossing all over. The up-and-down ones are longitude. The longitude lines look like the long sections of a peeled orange, because they go up and down between the north and south poles.

In the opposite direction are the latitudes. Some people call them parallels because the latitudes are all parallel and will never touch each other. My favorite is the equator, at 0° latitude. All the other latitudes are either north or south of the equator.

You can find any location in the whole world by knowing the exact longitude and latitude. All you do is look at the number in degrees north, south, east, or west. Where one longitude line crosses over a latitude line, that's your spot.